CW00672784

Under the Sea
Search and Find

ALLSORTED.

First published in 2023 by Allsorted Ltd WD19 4BG U.K.

Copyright © Noodle Juice Ltd 2023

Text by Noodle Juice 2022

Illustrations by Liza Lewis 2022

All rights reserved

Printed in China

A CIP catalogue record of this book is available from the British Library.

ISBN: 978-1-912295-77-7

1 3 5 7 9 10 8 6 4 2

FSC
www.fsc.org
MIX
Paper | Supporting
responsible forestry
FSC® C005748

This book is made from
FSC®-certified paper.
By choosing this book,
you help to take care of
the world's forests.
Learn more: www.fsc.org.

There are sea creatures galore in this sensational search and find activity book. Can you spot the clownfish swimming near the coral reef? Who's hiding in the rock pool? What about the anglerfish lighting up the dark sea?

With hundreds of things to spot in the amazing underwater scenes, will you be able to find them all? Use the spotter's guide at the back of the book to help you identify the creatures in each species.

Coral reef

Colourful tropical fish dart between the corals, searching for food and avoiding predators. Clownfish dive into sea anemones' stinging tentacles to hide.

There are ten different types of tropical fish in this scene. Can you spot them all?

Deep dark sea

Down in the depths, deep-sea vents spurt black clouds into the sea. The lack of light means that lots of weird and wonderful creatures create their own light using bioluminescence.

It's murky down in the depths. Can you spot the 12 strange creatures who live here?

Penguin colony

Penguins gather together in colonies. Mums and dads take it in turn to look after their penguin egg while the other one heads out to sea to catch fish.

There are five matching pairs of penguin in this scene. Can you identify them all?

9

Rock pool

At high tide, the sea comes in to cover the shore. Once the tide has gone out, water is trapped between the rocks to form rock pools. Crabs, molluscs and sea anemones live here.

See if you can find all of these creatures in and around the rock pool!

Underwater treasure

Thousands of wrecked ships dot the ocean floors.
Divers look for treasure while fish and other sea
creatures make the wreck their home.

There are ten sea creatures hiding in and
near the wreck. Can you spot them all?

Arctic seas

Walruses and seals live near the Arctic Circle. Their thick skin and layers of blubber protect them from the cold and the ice.

Dolphin school

Dolphins are friendly mammals who communicate with squeaks and whistles. They can remember an individual dolphin's squeak for a long time.

There are 12 sea creatures having fun with the dolphins. Can you spot them all?

Tropical fish

Angelfish dart through the coral as they search for food.
Blowfish expand when they see a threat in tropical waters.

Deep waters

Amazing sea creatures live at every depth of the ocean.
There are over 34,000 kinds of fish alone.

Can you spot the incredible sea
creatures who live here?

Ocean adventures

Larger fish, such as dolphins, sharks and whales, all track smaller fish as they swim through the ocean.

Can you find these 16 sea creatures in this scene?

Carribean island

Turtles come to lay their eggs on the sandy beach.
Large rocks hide robber crabs who hunt newly
hatched turtles. Seagulls dive to get their share.

There are six pairs of turtles in this scene. Can you identify them all?

Octopus games

Octopuses lurk on the seabed. They use their tentacles to help them cross the ocean floor and capture their prey.

How many octopus legs can you spot?
There are ten other creatures to find.

Sharks

Sleek and deadly, sharks power through the waves in search of their prey. Their rough skin and sharp teeth ensure only the fiercest sea creature, the orca, or killer whale, hunts them.

There are 14 different sharks for you to find.

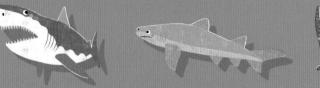

Seahorses

These delicate creatures float gently in the sea, changing colour to avoid detection. Their tails loop around seagrass to keep them in one place.

There are five matching pairs of seahorses in this scene. Can you identify them all?

31

Lobsters and crabs

Crustaceans such as lobsters and crabs are scattered all over the seabed. Their large pincers and hard shells help protect them from predators.

How many lobsters can you see? Can you spot these sea creatures too?

Ocean fish

Shoals of fish glisten in the sunlight as they swim
through the ocean. Tiny herring hope to hide
from predators using safety in numbers.

There are eight different kinds of fish in this scene and there's
an odd one out for each species. Can you spot them all?

Whales

From the huge sperm whale to the unicorn-like narwhal, the world's most impressive mammals swim majestically through the ocean.

There are eight matching pairs of
whales swimming in the scene.
Can you identify them?

Sea creature spotter's guide

Crab
crustacean; global
over 10,000 different species

blue crab

common hermit crab

Dungenesse crab

edible common crab

giant crab

king crab

pea crab

robber crab

sea spider

Tasmanian crab

white-spotted hermit crab

yeti crab

Dolphin
mammal; global
nearly 40 different species

Atlantic
spotted dolphin

Australian snubfin dolphin

bottlenose dolphin

common dolphin

Fraser's dolphin

grey dolphin

humpback
dolphin

Irrawaddy dolphin

Risso's dolphin

rough-toothed
dolphin

conger eel

Eel
teleost fish; global
over 800 different species

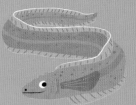

cutthroat eel

garden eel

gulper eel

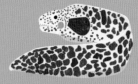

moray eel

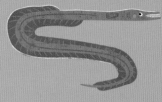

sawtooth eel

shortfin eel

snipe eel

spaghetti eel

snake eel

witch eel

Fish
marine vertebrate; global
over 34,000 different species

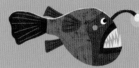

anglerfish

black swallower fish

blowfish

butterfly fish

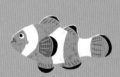

clownfish

cod

damsel fish

dragon fish

fangtooth fish

flashlight fish

flying fish

goby

lanternfish

Fish continued...

lionfish

loosejaw fish

mackerel

mandarin fish

Pacific regal blue tang

parrotfish

pilot fish

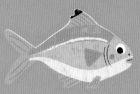
pony fish

rockling

royal angelfish

salmon

sardine

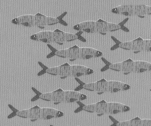
shoal of herring

swordfish

tuna

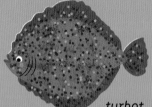
turbot

unicorn fish

viperfish

wolffish

yellow tang

big red jellyfish

Jellyfish
marine invertebrate; global
over 200 different species

box jellyfish

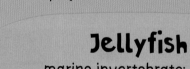
football jellyfish

lion's mane jellyfish

Cassiopea jellyfish

sea wasp jellyfish

American lobster

Lobster
crustacean; global
over 15 different species

common lobster

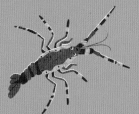

deep-sea lobster

European lobster

slipper lobster

spiny lobster

Octopus
mollusc; global shallow water
about 300 different species

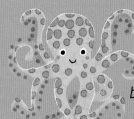

blue-ringed octopus

common octopus

day octopus

dumbo octopus

veined octopus

barnacles

Mollusc
mollusc; global
over 100,000 different species

clam

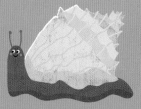

conch

lettuce slug

mussels

oyster

periwinkle

razor clam

scallops

whelk

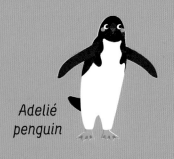

Adelié penguin

Penguin
flightless bird; Southern Hemisphere
between 18–21 different species

African penguin

blue or fairy penguin

chinstrap penguin

emperor penguin

Galapagos penguin

gentoo penguin

Humboldt penguin

king penguin

Magellanic penguin

rockhopper penguin

Seahorse
fish; shallow, global waters
about 50 different species

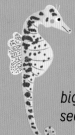

big-belly seahorse

Denise's pygmy seahorse

lined seahorse

Pacific seahorse

weedy seadragon

elephant seal

Seal
mammal; cold seas
32 different species

grey seal

harbour seal

harp seal

leopard seal

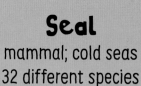

ribbon seal

ringed seal

Weddell seal

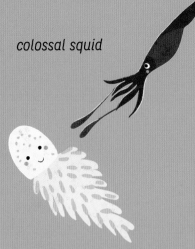
colossal squid

Squid
mollusc; global
over 300 different species

giant squid

Southern pygmy squid

siphonophore

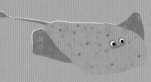
stingray

vampire squid

basking shark

Shark
fish; global
over 400 different species

blacktip reef shark

blue shark

cookiecutter shark

dwarf lantern shark

hammerhead shark

lemon shark

mako shark

nurse shark

pygmy shark

sand shark

spiny dogfish shark

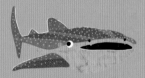
whale shark

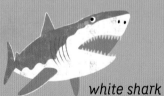
white shark

wobbigong
shark

Starfish
marine invertebrate; global
over 1,600 different species

bloody Henry starfish

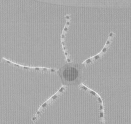
brittle starfish

crown-of-thorns
starfish
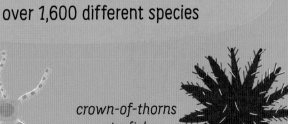

feather star

43

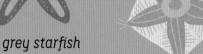

Starfish continued...

grey starfish

high Arctic starfish

sea cucumber

sunstar starfish

flatback turtle

Turtle
reptile; global except Antarctica
over 356 different species

green turtle

hawksbill turtle

Kemp's ridley turtle

leatherback turtle

loggerhead turtle

olive ridley turtle

Atlantic walrus

Walrus
mammal; Arctic seas
2 subspecies

Pacific walrus

beluga whale

Whale
mammal; global
about 40 different species

blue whale

bowhead whale

bottlenose whale

grey whale

humpback whale

killer whale

minke whale

narwhal

sperm whale

44

Search and find answers

Pages 4-5

Coral Reef

Pages 6-7

Deep dark sea

Pages 8-9

Penguin colony

Pages 10-11

Rock pool

Pages 12-13

Underwater treasure

Pages 14-15

Arctic seas

Pages 16-17

Dolphin school

Pages 18-19

Tropical fish

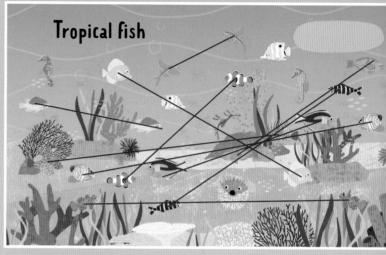

Pages 20-21

Deep waters

Pages 22-23

Ocean Adventures

Pages 24-25

Carribean island

Pages 26-27

Octopus games

There are 32 octopus legs.

46

Pages 28-29

Sharks

Pages 30-31

Seahorses

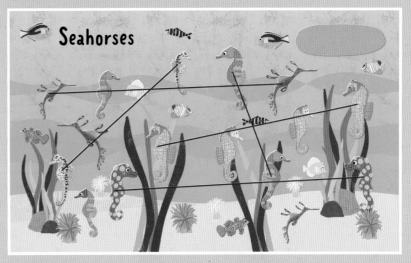

Pages 32-33

Lobsters and crabs

Pages 34-35

Ocean fish

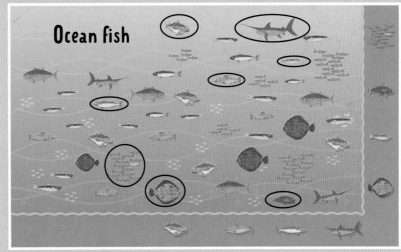

Pages 36-37

Whales

Pages 32-33
There are eight lobsters.